Muskrat Will Be Swimming

Written by Cheryl Savageau   Illustrated by Robert Hynes

Tilbury House ■ Publishers
Gardiner, Maine

The kids at school call us Lake Rats. And the place where we live, down by the lake's shore, they call Shanty Town. People at the lake live in cellar holes, trailers, and old winterized cottages from when the lake was a vacation spot for people with money. Now the lake is too crowded for vacationers. Now it's where we live.

I love the lake. I love the green, froggy smell of the pond out behind the dam. I love walking the shoreline every spring, watching for pollywogs. I love swimming in the strong, clean current at the point. I love fishing in the rain on early April mornings and sunny August afternoons. I love skating out past the islands in January, with stars thick over my head. But I don't like being called Lake Rat.

Mornings, I like getting up early to take my favorite path along the shore. In the gray light I can hear the sad-sounding call of a loon, and the scurrying of small animals I can't see. Ducks paddle close to shore, and across the water a great blue heron flies up and settles in an old pine tree. One morning, just before sunrise, I come to a turn in the path. Near a fallen log among the cattails a muskrat is preening herself in the early morning light. She turns and looks into my eyes, then dives into the water and swims away.

Sometimes, out running errands with my father, we drive past the big white houses uptown. The yards there are clean and clipped. None of them have prickly black raspberry bushes sprawling over the backyard. None of them have old cars to play in, or stacks of cement blocks someone might use someday, and none of the kids have clothes passed down from two sets of cousins. All their clothes are brand-new clean, not clean from hundreds of washings, faded and soft like mine. Sometimes I feel bad about the clothes. But I wouldn't want to live in their houses. Not if I had to live so far from the lake.

The truth is I love the lake. That's why it makes me so mad when they call us Lake Rats. Lake RATS. What do they know, anyway? I tried to tell them about the lake, what a great place it is to live. But they just laughed. "We wouldn't swim in that water," they said to me. "It's dirty, it smells. Bloodsuckers and snakes live in it."

I tried to tell them about the turtles laying eggs on the bank behind my aunt's house every spring. "How gross," they said. I told them about the dragonflies in summer, the bright blues, greens, and reds. "You Lake Rats are crazy." That's what they said to me. So I don't tell them about the fish we catch and eat at big fish-frys mid-summer under the stars. I figure they'd tell me food is supposed to come from the supermarket. So I just get quiet and don't say anything.

One night after supper Grampa notices me moping around.

"What's the matter, Jeannie?" he asks me. "What's got you so down?"

"Lake Rats," I tell him.

"Lake Rats?" he asks. "What are Lake Rats?"

"Lake Rats. That's what the kids at school call us."

"Oh, I see." Grampa sits down next to me on the stair. "Makes you feel kind of bad, huh?" I just nod my head.

"Come on, take a walk with me," he says. I follow him down the path to the place where the pond lilies grow the thickest. As we get closer, we can hear the bullfrogs' low voices, and the higher voices of the green frogs. We find a place to sit on an old log.

"Listen to those frogs," Grampa says. We both listen for awhile, and I almost forget about the Lake Rats thing. Then Grampa says, "When I was a kid, they called us Frogs. It was because we're part French. French and Indian, that's us. I don't know what frogs have to do with that, but that's what they called us. Frogs. Thought they'd hurt our feelings. Some people do that—when they want to make you feel bad, they compare you to an animal. We don't think that way. We know the animals are our relatives. We can learn a lot from them.

"See those frogs, that was us, puddle-jumpers, singers, people who always have something to say. They called me a frog because they thought it would hurt my feelings. That's because they didn't know frogs."

I think about what he says, and I listen to the frogs. Finally, I say, "I wouldn't mind being a frog like you. But Grampa, they call us Lake Rats. I don't want to be a Lake Rat.

"Well, what exactly is a Lake Rat, anyway?" Grampa asks.

"I don't know, but it sure sounds bad."

"That's because you haven't thought about it. Now, let's think about Lake Rats. Those kids who call you Lake Rat don't know about the lake the way you do. What kind of animal could it be, a Lake Rat?" I think with Grampa for awhile, and suddenly see in my mind the muskrat preening herself in the water, just as I'd seen her early one morning.

"A muskrat, Grampa," I say. At my words, I see the muskrat turn and look into my eyes, then dive into the water with hardly a ripple.

"That must be it," Grampa says. "Now, Muskrat is small, but important. It was Muskrat, remember, who brought earth up from the bottom of the water and put it on Turtle's back." As Grampa speaks, I remember him telling stories around the woodstove while we drank hot cocoa and wrapped ourselves in warm quilts, and the snow piled up outside.

A long, long time ago, the world was very different. There was water as far as you could see, in every direction. Only fish and water animals could live in this world. But way up in the sky, there was another world, with people walking around. There was a big tree in the middle of the sky world, with four white roots growing in the four directions. Wonderful flowers and fruits grew on the branches of that tree. One day the people pulled up the tree. A big hole opened in the sky where the tree had been. A woman, one who was curious, looked over the edge. She could see something glittering far below, like sun on the water. She held on to a branch of the tree and leaned over to get a better look. Suddenly, the branch broke and the woman fell, down through the hole in the sky.

The animals looked up and saw the Skywoman coming. They saw that she didn't look like them, that she couldn't live in the water— she didn't even have webbed feet! So two Swans flew up and caught her on their wings and began to bring her gently down to the world below.

The animals remembered that at the bottom of the water was something called earth. If they could bring some up, the woman would have something to stand on. So all the animals tried—the Duck, the Beaver with its strong legs, Loon with its powerful wings—but none of them could swim all the way to the bottom. Finally, a little voice said, "I will swim down and get earth, or I will die trying." It was Muskrat who said it. And Muskrat dove down into the water. Down, down, she swam into the dark, deep water. It felt as if her lungs would burst, but she kept swimming. Finally, her tiny paws scraped the bottom, and she let herself float back to the surface. All the animals were excited to see she had earth in her paw. But then they looked around at the surface of the water and said, "But where will we put it?"

That's when Turtle swam up and said, "You can put earth on my back." The Swans brought Skywoman down and she stepped onto Turtle's back. She dropped seeds from the tree in the sky, and they began to grow. And so the woman from the sky came to live on this earth on Turtle's back, and that's where we all live now.

"I do remember that story, Grampa," I tell him. We walk back home together, and I think about Muskrat.

That night I dive into the waters of my dream. My body is covered with fur, and I dive

down,

and down,

and down.

I feel as if my lungs will burst, but I keep on swimming. Finally, my paws scrape the bottom, and I shoot up through the water into the light. The sunlight is shining through my window. I get up and dress and go out to find Grampa.

"Let's go out on the lake, Grampa," I say. "There's something I have to do."

"Sounds pretty important," Grampa says, and walks with me down to the water. Grampa and I paddle, and I tell him about my dream.

"That's a good dream," he says. Finally, we stop paddling, and we sit quietly, listening and watching. Then I decide what to do. I take a deep breath.

"Watch me, Grampa," I yell, and dive over the side.

The water is cold, but I swim down and down, just like in my dream. It feels as if my lungs will burst, but I know I can do it. I kick as hard as I can, and finally my hands scrape the bottom and close over the soft mud. I turn, push off the bottom, and swim back into the light. Grampa is watching me over the side of the canoe. He reaches out to pull me in, and I put the earth into his hand. He places the wet earth carefully on the seat, then helps me into the canoe. "Come on, Muskrat," he says. "It's time for breakfast."

So I don't worry anymore when kids call me a Lake Rat. I know who I am, and I know about the lake, that we're part of it, and it's part of us. Grampa let the mud dry out and put it in a leather pouch for me so I can keep it always.

Tonight everyone will come to our house, and I'll play cards with my cousins on the bunk beds, and the grownups will play cards around the kitchen table. We'll eat stew or spaghetti and something made from the blueberries we picked on the island today. Later my mother will play the piano, one of my uncles will take up the guitar, and Grampa will play the drum, and we'll all sing together until the whole cellar hole is rocking.

Outside, the lake will lap against the shore while the moon looks down, and somewhere, Muskrat will be swimming.

Notes on the Story

In Native American cultures, stories have always been used to teach both children and adults. Family stories as well as traditional stories are told, and both are included in *Muskrat Will Be Swimming.* The Skywoman story is part of the creation story of the Haudenonsaunee, People of the Long House, also known as the Iroquois. The version retold here is from the Seneca, as told by Joseph Bruchac, and is used with his permission. Among the Iroquois, stories are traditionally told during the long winter season. For more stories of the Iroquois and other Native people, see *Iroquois Stories* and *Keepers of the Earth,* both by Joseph Bruchac.

Muskrats are water mammals related to the beaver. They live in marshes, lakes, swamps, and streams. Their coat is a mixture of short, soft underfur for insulation, and long, shiny guard hairs for protection from the water. Their tails are hairless and flattened, and their back feet are partially webbed.

In a marsh, lake, or swamp, muskrats build mound-shaped lodges of twigs, cattail stalks, grass, and mud. Inside the lodge, above the waterline, there is a dry room for a nest. Tunnels lead to underwater entrances or go underground and lead to entrances on the shore.

When young are born, the female stays with them in the warm, dry nest in the lodge, while the male lives in another nest outside the main lodge. At other times they live in mated pairs.

Muskrats like to eat plants such as cattails and grass and some fish and crayfish. Above the waters of the pond, they build feeding platforms, where they climb to eat their favorite foods. Great builders, they also make channels for swimming through the tall cattails and rushes, and on stream banks they make mud slides into the water. They usually stay underwater for just a few minutes, but can stay under for up to fifteen minutes in emergencies.

Muskrats are mostly nocturnal (nock-TUR-nal, meaning they are active mostly at night), but can also be seen at dawn and dusk. During the winter they sometimes come out during the day.

About the Author and Illustrator

Cheryl Savageau grew up a "lake rat" on the shores of a lake in Massachusetts, where she spent a lot of time swimming, canoeing, and walking the shoreline. She is French and Abenaki. She lives in New Hampshire now with her husband Bill and three cats, and has two grandchildren, Joe and Adam, who visit her several times a week. She is a poet, quilter, and storyteller, and teaches part-time at the University of New Hampshire in Durham.

Robert Hynes's two favorite subjects—natural history and art—wove together in his life at a very early age. When he finished his B.A. at the University of Maryland (where he also received his M.F.A.), he was asked by the Museum of Natural History in Washington, D.C., to paint the murals for its bicentennial celebration; these paintings launched his career. People from the National Geographic Society noticed the murals, and Robert has now illustrated several dozen adult and children's books for the Society. Robert lives in Rockville, Maryland, next to a stream and is often visited by deer, turtles, beaver, and, of course, muskrats.

For Teachers

Visit our website at www.tilburyhouse.com for suggestions on using this book in the classroom: activities, literature links, and further resources.

For Joe and Adam. —C. S.

To Buzz. —R. H.

TILBURY HOUSE, PUBLISHERS
103 Brunswick Avenue • Gardiner, Maine 04345 • 800–582–1899 • www.tilburyhouse.com

First paperback printing: March 2006 • 10 9 8 7 6 5 4 3 2

Library of Congress Cataloging-in-Publication Data
Savageau, Cheryl, 1950–
   Muskrat will be swimming / Cheryl Savageau ; illustrated by Robert Hynes.
      p. cm.
   Summary: A Native American girl's feelings are hurt when schoolmates make fun of the children who live at the lake, but then her grampa tells her a Seneca folktale that reminds her how much she appreciates her home and her place in the world.
   ISBN-13: 978-0-88448-280-2 (pbk. : alk. paper)
   ISBN-10: 0-88448-280-4 (pbk. : alk. paper)
   1. Seneca Indians--Juvenile fiction. [1. Seneca Indians--Fiction. 2. Indians of North America--Fiction. 3. Lakes--Fiction. 4. Grandfathers--Fiction. 5. Muskrat--Fiction. 6. Self-acceptance--Fiction.] I. Hynes, Robert, ill. II. title.
   PZ7.S2616Mu 2006
   [E]--dc22   2005029659

Production by Tilbury House, Publishers.
Printed by Sung In Printing, South Korea